The Catcher's Mask

To Ian Christopher

A Peach Street Mudders Story

The Catcher's Mask

by Matt Christopher

Illustrated by Bert Dodson

Little, Brown and Company
Boston New York Toronto London

First Edition

The characters and events portrayed in this book are fictitious.
Any similarity to real persons, living or dead, is coincidental
and not intended by the author.

Library of Congress Cataloging-in-Publication Data

Christopher, Matt.
    The catcher's mask : a Peach Street Mudders story / Matt
Christopher ; illustrated by Bert Dodson. — 1st ed.
        p.   cm.
    Summary: Mudders' catcher Rudy Calhoun is having a
bad season behind the plate until, at a yard sale, he buys a
used catcher's mask that greatly improves his playing.
    ISBN 0-316-14186-0
    [1. Baseball — Fiction.   2. Catchers (Baseball) — Fiction.]
I. Dodson, Bert, ill.   II. Title.
PZ7.C458Cat   1997
[Fic] — dc21   97-40052

                    10 9 8 7 6 5 4 3 2 1

                                    WOR

Published simultaneously in Canada
by Little, Brown & Company (Canada) Limited

Printed in the United States of America

1

Rudy looked at the wall clock next to the kitchen cabinet. *Five of three. I should be leaving,* he thought. *Most of the guys will be warming up already. Zero's probably wondering where I am.*

His mother came in from the living room and glanced at the clock.

"Don't you think you'd better take off?" she said.

"I guess so," Rudy mumbled. He put on his baseball cap and picked up his catcher's mitt.

His mother smiled sadly. "Rudy, I know you don't think you've been playing well lately," she said, guessing what had him down in the mouth. "But everybody makes mistakes. I'm sure you'll improve before you know it."

Rudy nodded. She was right about his poor playing. But he didn't think she was right about his getting better.

Rudy stepped out the door and hurried to the garage, where he kept his bike. He strapped his glove to the back carrier, put on his bike helmet, and pedaled off.

Every Peach Street Mudder was there when Rudy arrived at the field.

"Glad you could make it, Calhoun," Coach Parker said sarcastically. "Go help Zero warm up."

"Shoot," muttered Chess Laveen. Chess, a stocky boy, was the team's substitute catcher. "Thought I'd get to start for a change."

Rudy didn't know what to say. He had half expected Coach Parker to start Chess at today's game. In fact, he almost wished he would. That way, Rudy wouldn't risk flubbing up, like he had the past few games.

The errors he had made during those games weren't terrible. Rudy just wasn't used to making mistakes, that's all. What was worse, he didn't know how to stop himself from making them.

After both teams had their infield, outfield, and batting practices, the High Street Bunkers took the field and the Peach Street Mudders took their first bats.

Barry McGee led off with a single. Then he advanced to second on Turtleneck Jones's sacrifice bunt. He stayed there when José Mendez's high fly ball to center field was caught. But then he scored on T.V. Adams's double.

That was it. Nicky Chong struck out.

The scoreboard read Mudders 1, Bunkers 0.

Not a bad way to start a game, Rudy thought as he put on his catcher's gear. *I wonder if I can help keep the score reading like that. I doubt it.*

2

Pitching for the Mudders was Zero Ford, one of the best lefties in the league — usually. He started off by putting two strikes over the plate on Fuzzy McCormick. Then he gave Fuzzy a free ticket to first base.

"Rats," Rudy mumbled, thumping the inside of his mitt with his fist. He took a moment to readjust his catcher's mask. It had slipped, making it hard for him to see.

Sure wish I had my own mask, Rudy thought for the hundredth time. *This one stinks. Heck, it's probably the reason I'm screwing up all the time!*

But he knew that getting a new mask was impossible. Catcher's masks cost money, and he didn't have a lot of that. And as long as the Mudders had one he could use, his parents didn't see why he needed his own.

Ron Bush, the Bunkers' second batter, took two called strikes, then belted one over short-stop Bus Mercer's head for a single. Fuzzy stopped at second.

The next batter popped out. Then Alec Frost, the cleanup hitter, waited out a 3–2 count and smacked a double between left and center fields.

As José raced to catch it, Fuzzy McCormick rounded third and headed toward home. Rudy leaped to his feet and threw off his mask, his heart thumping as he waited for José's throw-in.

The ball came in a little too high. Keeping his eye glued to it, Rudy took a few steps back to catch it. But he stumbled on something and fell.

By the time he looked up, Fuzzy was crossing home plate.

"Have a nice *trip!* Guess we'll see you next *fall!*" Fuzzy laughed hard at his own joke.

Red in the face, Rudy stood up and brushed the dirt off his uniform. Then he saw what had tripped him. It was his catcher's mask!

Darn this mask! he thought angrily as he picked it up and tugged it into place. *Bet I would have had that one if this stupid thing hadn't gotten in my way. Then that Fuzzy wouldn't be laughing.*

With Alec standing up at second and Ron on third, Andy Campbell, the Bunkers' next hitter, came up to the plate. He creamed Zero's first pitch for a home run over the left field fence. That really gave the Bunkers' fans something to scream about.

The Mudders fans weren't silent, either. "How about giving your pitcher a pep talk, catcher?" someone in the crowd yelled. "Or don't you know that's part of your job?"

Rudy did know that. But he usually joined Coach Parker at the mound. He had never gone out on his own before. And he wasn't about to try it now.

He didn't have to. Zero seemed to muster his strength. He struck out the next hitter, and the next one flied out to end the inning.

The score read Bunkers 4, Mudders 1.

Alfie Maples, leading off the top of the second inning for the Mudders, laced Alec Frost's third pitch for a single over short. Rudy was on deck, swinging his bat, when Bus Mercer flied out.

Rudy walked to the plate, heart pounding. He tried to forget how he had tripped in front of the crowd. But Fuzzy's mocking remark was still ringing in his ears. More than anything, he wanted to get a hit.

"C'mon, Rudy! C'mon, kid! Wallop that ball!"

The cries from the Mudders' bench boosted

him a little. Then Alec put two strikes by him, and he fanned at the third. Rudy walked back to the bench, dragging his feet in the dirt.

Zero belted out a single, advancing Alfie to second. But neither boy made it home because Barry McGee flied out.

Fortunately, the Bunkers didn't add any more runs during their next raps. But neither did the Mudders. The bottom of the third inning started with the score still 4–1.

Rudy crouched down behind the plate and waited for Zero's pitch. He was perspiring hard underneath all his catcher's equipment. The upper pad of the catcher's mask rubbed painfully on his sweaty forehead. He glanced over at the water jug and thought of how great it would feel to duck his head under a stream of cold water.

A movement on the mound snapped his attention back to the game. Zero's pitch was rocketing at him! The Bunker batter swung hard and missed. Rudy moved to make the catch. Too late! He chased the ball as it rebounded off the backstop.

Catcalls and laughter came from the Bunkers' bench.

"Caught napping, Calhoun?" Rudy heard Fuzzy McCormick's voice loud and clear.

Rudy scowled. *I just want this game to be over!* he thought.

Luckily the Bunkers went down quickly.

Coach Parker gave his team a quick pep talk that must have worked. The first two batters, Nicky and Alfie, got on base. As Bus strode to the plate, Rudy stood up to move to the on-deck circle.

"Rudy," Coach Parker called, "I'm subbing Chess in for you. Your mind just doesn't seem to be on the game today."

Rudy returned to his place on the bench. *I blew it again. It's all because of that stupid catcher's mask!* he thought with despair. *I'd be a much better player if it wasn't for that lousy piece of equipment.*

3

The game ended with the Mudders losing to the Bunkers 4–1. As usual, Rudy was one of the last ones to leave the bench area. He had to help Chess pack up the catcher's equipment and carry it to the coach's car. After it was loaded in, Rudy gave the bag a punch.

"Stupid stuff," he muttered under his breath. Chess gave him a funny look but didn't say anything. Moments later, Rudy was on his bike, pedaling for home.

When he rounded the corner of his street, he had to brake quickly to keep from smashing into a parked car. In fact, there were a lot of parked cars lining both sides of the road.

What's going on? Rudy wondered. He swung off his bike and walked with it down the street. He stopped in front of the Turnballs' house and stared.

The lawn was covered with stuff: chairs, tables, boxes of books and magazines, lamps, pictures, even a toaster and a telephone. People were inspecting items, and Rudy saw a few of them carry their choices to a table set up to one side. Behind the table sat Mrs. Turnball. The people handed her money, then walked away with their purchases.

Rudy had seen yard sales before, but he'd never stopped at one. He was curious. Maybe if he saw something he liked, he could bike home and get some money to buy it.

He leaned his bike against a tree and joined the other people milling around the lawn. He poked into a few of the book boxes but didn't see anything he wanted to read. He picked up a funny-looking lamp, but the cord at the end was frayed and he wasn't sure his mom or dad would know how to fix it. He wasn't interested in ashtrays or old plates and glasses. In fact, he didn't see anything he really liked. He turned to leave.

Just then, he spotted something sticking out of a box that was jammed under a table. He tugged the box free and pulled the thing out.

It was a catcher's mask — and though it looked like an older model, it was in good condition. Rudy could tell at a glance that it was smaller than the one he used during the Mudders' games. He slipped it over his head. Even without the protective helmet he'd have to wear underneath it, he knew it fit perfectly.

"Hello, Rudy. Find something you like?" Rudy looked up to see Mr. Turnball standing beside him. Rudy pulled off the mask.

"Sure did. How much does it cost?" Rudy replied.

Mr. Turnball took the mask from him. "Well, now, let's see." He frowned. "Hmm, I don't remember this. Wonder where it came from."

He examined it a little longer, then handed it back to Rudy. "Looks like someone marked his initials on it. *Y.B.* Can't say as I know anyone with those initials. Tell you what: you can have it for two dollars."

He reached into a box beside him, rummaged around for a moment, then came out with a book. *Play Ball!* the cover read. He glanced around and lowered his voice. "I'll throw this old book in, too. Mrs. Turnball says anything that doesn't get sold today gets hauled to the dump. I'd just as soon know that my old books are being read rather than sitting at the bottom of a trash heap."

Rudy grinned and thanked Mr. Turnball. He hurried home, emptied out his piggy bank, and pulled out a five-dollar bill. He returned to the Turnballs' as fast as he could. Mr. Turnball gave him three dollars in change, and Rudy left, the proud owner of a new catcher's mask and a book.

4

That night after dinner, Rudy lay on the living room floor and looked through his new book. It was filled with pictures of famous baseball players and lots of advice about how to play different positions. Rudy turned to the section on catching.

The catcher is one of the most important players in the game, the book said. *He is the only member of the team who faces the field. Therefore, he's the only one who can see what's going on at every position. A smart catcher can help his team a lot by keeping them informed of what he sees.*

Rudy glanced at the catcher's mask beside him. *Well, I'll be able to see a lot more out there now that I have a mask that fits!* he said to himself.

He turned the page. There was a big black-and-white photo of a catcher diving for a pop-up. In the corner was the player's signature. Rudy recognized the name right away.

Lawrence "Yogi" Berra gives everything he's got to make the play, the words beneath the photo read.

Lawrence Peter Berra was born on April 12, 1925. He got his nickname, "Yogi," when a friend who had seen a movie of a Hindu practicing yoga told him that's what he looked like.

Yogi — now that's a name a guy isn't likely to forget, Rudy thought with a smile. *And he was a catcher, just like me.*

He continued reading about the famous catcher. He learned that Yogi Berra had been on ten World Series Championship teams.

He had played for almost twenty years, from 1946 to 1965, and was named Most Valuable Player three times. After he retired as a player, he managed two New York major league teams. Rudy wasn't at all surprised to learn that Yogi Berra had been elected to the Baseball Hall of Fame.

He stared at the famous catcher's picture and signature. Suddenly something Mr. Turnball had said that afternoon flashed in his mind: "Someone marked his initials on it. Y.B."

Rudy snatched up the mask. Sure enough, there were the initials, plain as day!

Rudy looked at the initials, then at the signature in the book, and back again. His heart started pounding. To his eye, the *Y* and the *B* on the mask looked exactly the same as the *Y* and the *B* on the photograph!

Yogi Berra signed this catcher's mask! he thought excitedly. *I bet it's really valuable!*

Then another thought struck him. If it was

valuable, would he have to give it back to Mr. Turnball? After all, he had paid Mr. Turnball only two dollars for it. He might not want Rudy to have it if it was worth a lot of money.

He knew he should tell Mr. Turnball what he'd found out about the initials. But he didn't want to. He didn't care if the mask might be worth a lot of money, although that was exciting. No, Rudy wanted to keep it because he was sure he'd be the best catcher in the league if he played with a Hall-of-Famer's mask.

He slipped the mask over his face.

I'll just play one game with it, Rudy thought, staring at the photo of Yogi Berra. *After all, Mr. Turnball couldn't remember where the mask came from. And he saw the initials himself, so it's not like I'm hiding anything from him.*

With that, he pushed away his guilty thoughts and started to read the book again.

5

When Rudy woke up the next morning, the first thing he saw was the catcher's mask on his nightstand. The second thing he saw was the baseball book. Before he had turned out his light the night before, he had read the chapter on catching twice.

Rudy pushed the book aside and picked up the mask. The book had been interesting to read. But he already knew that a catcher had to be strong enough to throw a runner out at second. And that he had to have good balance and quick reflexes to chase after bunts, field pop fouls, and snap up wild pitches. And that the catcher had to be brave, especially when a runner was coming in full steam ahead from third.

No, it wasn't reading a book about catching that was going to make him a better player. It was the mask. After all, it had belonged to one of the best catchers in the game, hadn't it? He couldn't wait to try it out.

That afternoon, he got his wish. Sparrow Fisher called to say that Coach Parker wanted to hold a practice.

"We're playing the Bearcats on Thursday. He thinks we need to bone up a little before then," Sparrow said. Although he didn't say it, Rudy felt sure that Sparrow thought Rudy needed the extra practice more than anyone.

Well, we'll see about that, Rudy thought.

"You're here bright and early," said Nicky Chong as Rudy rode up a few hours later. "Lately, you've been the last one at the field."

Rudy just grinned and asked Nicky to help him on with his catcher's equipment. When

Nicky tried to hand him the Mudders' catcher's mask, Rudy shook his head.

"I've got my own now," he said, proudly holding up the *Y.B.* mask.

Nicky examined it, then shrugged. "Looks kind of old and scruffy," he said. "But as long as you can catch with it, who cares?"

"Oh, you can bet on that!" Rudy replied positively. He was going to tell Nicky about the initials but suddenly decided not to. For now, he wanted to keep it a secret that he was playing with a mask that had once belonged to a Hall-of-Famer.

Okay, Yogi, let's show them what we can do, he thought as he slid the mask into place.

Rudy hurried behind the plate. Sparrow Fisher was on the mound for the Mudders.

"Okay, fellas," Coach Parker called, "let's do a few quick drills, then we'll have a little infield practice. Once around the horn to begin."

Sparrow started the drill by hurling the ball to Rudy. Rudy threw the ball to first base. Turtleneck Jones sent it rocketing to Nicky at second. Nicky hurled it to T.V. Adams at third, who relayed it back to Rudy.

"All right! Good throws, guys!" Rudy called. He had never felt better during a warm-up. He was raring to start the scrimmage.

"Okay, Mudders, no mistakes, no mistakes!"

Barry McGee came to the plate. "Sheesh, you're a real loudmouth today, Rudy," he said. "What's come over you?"

Rudy grinned through his mask. "It's what's come over my *face* that's making the difference," he said mysteriously.

Barry stared at him, shrugged, then turned to face Sparrow.

Sparrow's first pitch was in the dirt in front of home plate. Barry jumped out of the way.

But Rudy didn't even flinch. He snagged the ball before it had a chance to rebound into the backstop.

"Nice stop, Rudy. Guess what's over your face is helping," Barry complimented him. He faced Sparrow again and this time got a good pitch, which he sent through the grass toward first.

José Mendez took a turn at bat next and hit a bouncing grounder toward second.

Nicky fielded José's hit cleanly and stepped on the bag to get Barry out. But he bumbled the throw to first and missed making the double play.

"That's okay, Nicky. Save it for the game instead!" Rudy yelled from behind the plate. Nicky waved to show he'd heard.

Alfie Maples was up next. The coach said a few words to him. Then Alfie adjusted his glasses and stepped to the plate. He let two of Sparrow's pitches go by. Then, on the third, he suddenly squared his shoulders, slid his top hand toward the fat part of the bat, and tried to lay down a bunt.

The ball bounced a few feet in front of the plate. Alfie took off to first. José motored to second.

But Rudy was in motion, too. He scooped up the ball and hurled it to second base just as José prepared to hit the dirt.

Nicky caught it and whipped his glove around and down to tag José. José's slide was good, but thanks to Rudy's accurate throw, Nicky's tag was better. José was out.

The play didn't stop there, though. Alfie Maples still hadn't touched first base.

"Double play! Double play!" Rudy screamed.

Nicky rifled the ball to Turtleneck just in time to get Alfie out.

"All right!" Rudy cried.

Coach Parker had substitutes Tootsie Malone and Jack Livingston take a rap, then went through the order two more times.

Even though it was just a practice, Rudy kept a sharp eye on everything that was going on. Once, he caught Tootsie taking a big lead off first. He suspected Tootsie, a speedy runner, was going to steal second. Sure enough, as Sparrow completed his windup, Tootsie took off.

Rudy had already jumped up. He caught the ball and rocketed it to Nicky. Tootsie was out by a mile.

Shortly after that, Coach Parker called it quits.

"Good practice, guys. Rudy, I haven't seen you play so well in a while. I don't know what brought on the sudden change, but keep it up!" The coach went on to compliment each of the other boys or to point out instances where they could improve.

Rudy grinned from ear to ear. He peeked at the mask in his lap.

It worked! he thought gleefully. *Thanks, Yogi Berra, wherever you are!*

6

Two days later, the Mudders faced the Bearcats.

The Bearcats were up first. Rudy crouched behind the plate, ready for action, *Y.B.* mask in place. He could hardly wait for the first pitch.

The Bearcats' catcher, Jimmy Sullivan, led off for his team. Jimmy was husky and muscular for a ten-year-old. He could deliver the ball a mile if he connected squarely.

That's just what he did this time. On Sparrow's third pitch, Jimmy sent the ball to deep left center field. José couldn't get to it before it hit the ground, and Jimmy made it safely to second.

That's where he stayed for a while. A pop fly to short and a grounder to second made it two outs for the Bearcats.

Then Bus fumbled a snake-sizzling grounder to short. The batter, Stretch Ferguson, made it to first, and Jimmy advanced to third.

Rudy sized up the situation. "Okay, guys, the play is to second or first," he shouted. "We only need one!"

Horace Robb sent a scorching double to Barry McGee's right side, scoring Jimmy and planting Stretch safely on third.

Finally, Jack Walker grounded out to second. The Bearcats led, 1-0.

Sadly, the Peach Street Mudders did nothing their turn at bat.

Bearcat Boots Finkle came up to bat in the

top of the second. Sparrow tried hard, but Boots got on first safely. Then Luke Bonelle came up.

Rudy squatted behind the plate. Suddenly he realized that Luke might try a sacrifice bunt to send Boots to second base.

He shifted his position slightly and prepared himself to spring into action.

Sparrow went through his windup and let the ball go. Sure enough, Luke squared himself around and bunted. The ball dribbled forward, and Luke took off for first like a scared rabbit.

But Rudy was already in motion. He scrambled forward, plucked up the ball, and heaved it to Turtleneck. Turtleneck lunged to meet the throw just as Luke was nearing first. The ball socked into Turtleneck's glove a split second before Luke hit the base.

"Out!" the umpire cried. But hardly anyone heard him. From his position, Rudy had seen Boots Finkle stumble on his way to second. If

Turtleneck threw quickly, they might be able to get Boots out, too.

"Second! Second!" Rudy yelled at the top of his lungs.

Turtleneck immediately hurled the ball to Nicky. Nicky stretched, snagged the throw, and swept his glove around in time to tag Boots.

"Out!" came the second-base umpire's call.

The Mudders' fans went wild. They were still cheering when Jim Jakes flied out to José to end the half inning.

Coach Parker was all smiles as the Mudders ran in from the field.

"Nice double play, guys," he said, clapping his hands. "Good eyes, Rudy. That's the kind of smarts catchers need to have. Keep up the good work."

Rudy grinned and slid his mask from his face. "Oh, I don't think that will be a problem, Coach. Nope, not a problem at all."

7

The Mudders took their raps, but again their bats were silent. Going into the third inning, the score still read Bearcats 1, Mudders 0.

Rudy suited up and headed for the plate, carrying his mitt.

"Okay, Bearcats, look out! We're going to stop you cold!" he cried out.

"Fat chance," said Jimmy Sullivan, the Bearcats' leadoff batter. "Your pitcher is getting tired."

It seemed that Jimmy was right. Sparrow threw three pitches, all bad.

"Time!" Rudy called. He yanked off his

helmet and trotted to the mound. "Take your time, take your time," he advised Sparrow. "I'm giving you a nice big target here" — he held up his mitt — "and all you have to do is hit it."

"I'm doing my best," Sparrow mumbled.

"I know, but I'm going to help you do better." He leaned close to Sparrow. "I've noticed that that clown Jimmy has trouble judging pitches that are low and outside. Think you can put one there?"

Sparrow grinned. "I'll try."

Rudy turned to go, but Sparrow called him back. "Hey, you know this is the first time you've ever come out to the mound without the coach?"

Rudy realized that Sparrow was right. "Well, I have a feeling it won't be the last time. That okay with you?"

"I'll tell you after I see if a low-and-outside pitch works!"

Rudy jogged back to his position. Crouching low, he held his glove up nice and wide.

"Hey, Jimmy, why don't you take a swing at the next one? C'mon, what've you got to lose? Or are you afraid you'll miss?" Rudy goaded the batter.

"I'll show you," Jimmy shot back. "I'll send this one out of the park!"

Sparrow went through his windup and delivered. It was a perfect low-and-outside pitch.

Sure enough, Jimmy cut at it as hard as he could. He missed by a mile.

"Strike!" yelled the umpire.

"Two more just like that, Sparrow, two more like that!" Rudy yelled. And in a voice just loud enough for the batter to hear, he added, "Two more just like that, Jimmy!"

Jimmy growled, but two pitches later, he was stalking back to the Bearcats' bench. He glared at Rudy over his shoulder.

"Just you wait until you're at bat — you and all your Mudder teammates," he hissed.

Rudy just smiled.

Drew Zellar was up next. He hit the first pitch to right center field. Alfie Maples tried to make the catch but fumbled the ball. Drew stood up at second.

Buck Austin walked. Players at first and second. Stretch came to the plate. He walloped Sparrow's third pitch head-high down the first base line. It looked like a sure single. The runners took off.

But at the last moment, Turtleneck Jones stuck out his glove and caught the ball! Buck Austin tried to get back to first, but he was too late. Turtleneck landed smack on the base, and Buck was out.

The Mudders' fans cheered as the team jogged in from the field.

The score was still Bearcats 1, Mudders 0.

8

"Okay, okay, let's see some good hitting out there!" Coach Parker yelled. It was the bottom of the third inning, and Rudy knew that the coach wanted them to get on the scoreboard.

Rudy took off his equipment and laid everything but the mask in a pile. The mask he held on to tightly.

Turtleneck was up first. He took three swings, all foul balls. The fourth pitch was wild. So were the next three. Turtleneck had a free ride to first.

Next up was José. Sometimes José hit well; other times he struck out.

Today was one of the strikeout days. José returned to the bench and tossed his helmet aside angrily.

"That's okay, José," Rudy said consolingly. "Everybody makes outs."

"I'm not mad about that," José replied. "I'm mad because of what that Jimmy Sullivan said while I was up. He called the Mudders losers and said we'd have better luck playing against five-year-olds in T-ball. That guy really gets me steamed!"

Rudy nodded. He wasn't surprised that Jimmy was bad-mouthing the batters. But he didn't tell José that he, Rudy, had started it. Instead, he decided he'd cool it the next time he was behind the plate. After all, he didn't want to do anything that might hurt his team.

If Jimmy Sullivan said anything nasty to T.V. Adams, T.V. apparently didn't let it bother him. He swung at the first pitch and made it on base. Turtleneck advanced safely to second. Suddenly it looked like the Mudders had a chance to score a run.

Then Nicky hit a shallow pop fly. The Bearcats' second baseman took one step back and caught it. Two outs.

Alfie Maples was up next.

"C'mon, Alfie, you can do it!" Rudy yelled. But he didn't really believe that. Alfie usually got out.

This time was no exception. Although Alfie connected with the ball, it dribbled down the first base line. Bearcats pitcher Stretch Ferguson fielded it easily and sent it to the first baseman for the out.

"Rats," Rudy said. He worked his way into his gear and walked to the plate.

Three batters later, he was walking back to the bench. Sparrow had found his stride and was pitching like a big leaguer.

Unfortunately so was Stretch Ferguson. Bus, Rudy, and Sparrow all struck out.

"You losers didn't even last long enough for me to open my mouth," Jimmy Sullivan crowed as he passed Rudy. "I got to sit back and watch you dig yourselves into a deeper hole!"

Rudy seethed but held his tongue. Then the Bearcats went down one, two, three, with Jimmy making the third out. Rudy couldn't stop himself.

"Funny, I don't hear anything coming from your mouth now," he called to the Bearcats' catcher.

"Yeah, well, one look at the scoreboard shows who the winners of this game are gonna be," Jimmy shot back.

"C'mon, c'mon, let's get cracking," Coach Parker interrupted. "It's the bottom of the fifth. Let's give our fans something to cheer about — what do you say?"

The Mudders all shouted their agreement.

Barry McGee followed through on the coach's instructions. He sent Stretch

Ferguson's fourth pitch over the fence for a home run. Suddenly it was a tie ball game, 1–1.

Turtleneck Jones helped by hitting a double. Then José redeemed himself by socking a single. Turtleneck wisely stayed on second.

T.V. shouldered the bat and narrowed his eyes at the Bearcats' pitcher. Rudy could tell he wanted nothing more than to send both Turtleneck and José home.

He didn't. He struck out.

But Nicky came through with a shallow pop fly that fell behind the second baseman and in front of the center fielder. Turtleneck's legs churned up the dirt as he rounded third and headed for home.

The center fielder got his hands on the ball and heaved it to Jimmy. The Mudders were on their feet, screaming for Turtleneck to slide.

Turtleneck did. Jimmy caught the throw, swept his glove around — and dropped the ball!

45

Turtleneck was safe, and the Mudders had the lead!

Even though Alfie hit into a double play, the Mudders were all smiles as they took to the field. Rudy didn't say a word as he passed Jimmy. He didn't have to. From the look on Jimmy's face, he knew Jimmy was yelling at himself for his error.

Well, I know what that's like, Rudy thought, feeling just the tiniest bit sorry for the other catcher.

The Bearcats were fired up at the top of the sixth and final inning. They seemed determined to take back their lead. If they succeeded, the Mudders would have to win the game with their last raps. But if they failed, the game would end right then with the Mudders victorious.

Rudy tugged his Hall-of-Famer mask into place.

Okay, Yogi, he said to himself, *let's see what we can do to end this game early!*

9

Drew Zellar was up first for the Bearcats. He hit a clean single.

"That's okay, guys, that's okay!" Rudy called. "The play is to first or second, first or second. Heck, let's make it to first *and* second for the double play!"

The crowd chuckled.

Buck Austin quieted them, however, when he laid down a perfect bunt. It was closer to Sparrow than to Rudy, so Rudy shouted for Sparrow to take it. Sparrow did, and tried to get Drew out at second. But Nicky flubbed the play, and Drew sped on to third!

Rudy looked up to see who the next batter for the Bearcats was. It was Stretch Ferguson, a good hitter. But Stretch wasn't walking to the plate yet. He was talking with the Bearcats' coach.

The coach patted Stretch on the back and sent him to the plate. Stretch stood outside the batter's box for a moment, running his hands up and down the bat and adjusting his helmet.

Stretch looks nervous, Rudy thought, puzzled. He glanced at the field, sizing up the situation.

There are no outs. Buck might try to steal second. But why would that make Stretch nervous? All he has to do is make it hard for me to get off a good throw to Nicky.

Then Rudy's gaze fell on third base. He caught the Bearcats' third-base coach whispering to Drew.

What's he saying? Rudy wondered as he watched Drew slowly nod. He was even more puzzled when he saw Drew shift his position.

He looks like he's getting ready to run. But he's not going to be forced to move because there isn't a runner at second.

Right at that moment, Stretch stepped into the batter's box — and suddenly Rudy realized what was about to happen.

They're going to try to fake us out with a suicide squeeze play!

Rudy had just read about the squeeze play in the baseball book Mr. Turnball had given him. On the play, the batter bunted the ball in front of the plate halfway between the catcher and the pitcher. The runner at first took off for second, the batter took off for first — and the runner at third, hoping that the catcher and pitcher would field the ball in the traditional manner and throw to second or first, ran as fast as he could for home! If the play worked, they would earn a run and still have at least one runner on base.

It all depended on the batter laying down the perfect bunt — and the catcher being fooled into making the play to first or second.

No wonder Stretch is nervous. But they're not fooling me! Rudy could scarcely contain his excitement. *I'm ready for them. Oh, boy, am I ready for them!*

Sparrow reared back and threw. Just as Rudy suspected, Drew and Buck took off as fast as they could. Stretch tried to bunt.

The minute Stretch's bat met the ball, Rudy knew the Bearcats were in big trouble. Instead of sending the ball into the dirt, Stretch popped it a few feet straight up into the air!

Rudy threw off his mask and lunged forward. *Plop!* The ball landed smack in the middle of his glove. One out!

But Rudy didn't stop there. Drew and Buck hadn't counted on his making the catch. They were still running.

That was all Rudy needed. He fired a throw to T.V. at third, praying that T.V. was ready to catch it.

He was! He stepped on the bag in plenty of time to get Drew out.

By now, the fans were screaming. Rudy was yelling at the top of his lungs, too, but not with happiness. He was yelling instructions for T.V.

10

"First! First! Throw to first!"

T.V. reared back and threw a bullet to Turtleneck.

Rudy held his breath. Buck was a fast runner and was already on his way back to the bag. Would T.V.'s throw beat him?

Turtleneck reached out as far as he could, his toe still on the base. Buck's arms and legs pumped hard. Then he launched himself into a slide. The ball soared past him and socked into Turtleneck's glove. Turtleneck flashed his glove downward.

A cloud of dust rose around first base. For

a moment, Rudy couldn't see what was happening. Then he heard the first-base umpire's call.

"Out!"

The fans went wild. A triple play!

The Mudders charged in from the field, laughing and cheering. They swarmed around Rudy. Coach Parker's face was wreathed in smiles.

"I wouldn't have believed it unless I saw it with my own eyes," he said. "A triple play! Not bad, fellas, not bad at all."

"And we have Rudy to thank for it," Nicky pointed out. "He was on that bunt like he knew it was coming!"

"I did!" Rudy crowed. He picked up his catcher's mask and pointed to the initials. "When you play with a piece of equipment that once belonged to a Hall-of-Famer, there's not much you can't do!"

Coach Parker's eyes widened. "Let me see that, Rudy," he said.

Suddenly Rudy's good mood left him. Reluctantly he handed the mask to the coach.

Me and my big mouth, he thought. *Coach Parker will take Yogi's mask from me and give it back to Mr. Turnball for sure! There goes my game again.*

Coach Parker examined the mask for a moment, then, with a funny look on his face, asked Rudy where he got it. Rudy told him.

The coach grinned. "You think this is Yogi Berra's mask, don't you, Rudy? And you think that's why you've been playing better, right?"

Rudy nodded.

"Well, I hate to disappoint you, son. But I know this mask. It belonged to a high-school teammate of mine. His name was Roger Bilkins. But we called him 'You Bet' Bilkins, because whenever we asked him if he was going to catch a good game, he answered, 'You bet!' He was always losing things — that's why he put his initials on everything he owned." Coach Parker laughed. "I guess he lost this mask, anyway. Wonder how it ended up in Mr. Turnball's garage sale. Guess that'll always be a mystery!"

He handed the mask back to Rudy.

"So it's not a Hall-of-Famer's mask?" Rudy asked, disappointed.

Coach Parker's eyes twinkled. "Well, now, I guess we can't say for sure. I mean, it isn't one now, but who knows? You might want to sign it yourself. Maybe someday in the future, this mask *will* have belonged to a Hall-of-Famer — you!"

Rudy turned the mask around in his hands. He could see the perfect spot for his signature. He looked up at the coach.

"You really think I could make it to the Hall of Fame someday?"

The coach grinned and ruffled Rudy's hair. "After the game you played today? You bet!"

A
Peach Street
Mudders
Story

The action-packed Peach Street Mudders series by Matt Christopher:

All-Star Fever
The Catcher's Mask *
Centerfield Ballhawk
The Hit-Away Kid
Man Out at First
Shadow Over Second
The Spy on Third Base
Stranger in Right Field *
Zero's Slider

Join the Matt Christopher Fan Club!

To get your official membership card, the Matt Christopher *Sports Pages,* and a handy bookmark, send a business-size (9½" x 4") self-addressed, stamped envelope and $1.00 (in cash or a check payable to Little, Brown and Company) to:

Matt Christopher Fan Club
c/o Little, Brown and Company
3 Center Plaza
Boston, MA 02108

*Available in hardcover only